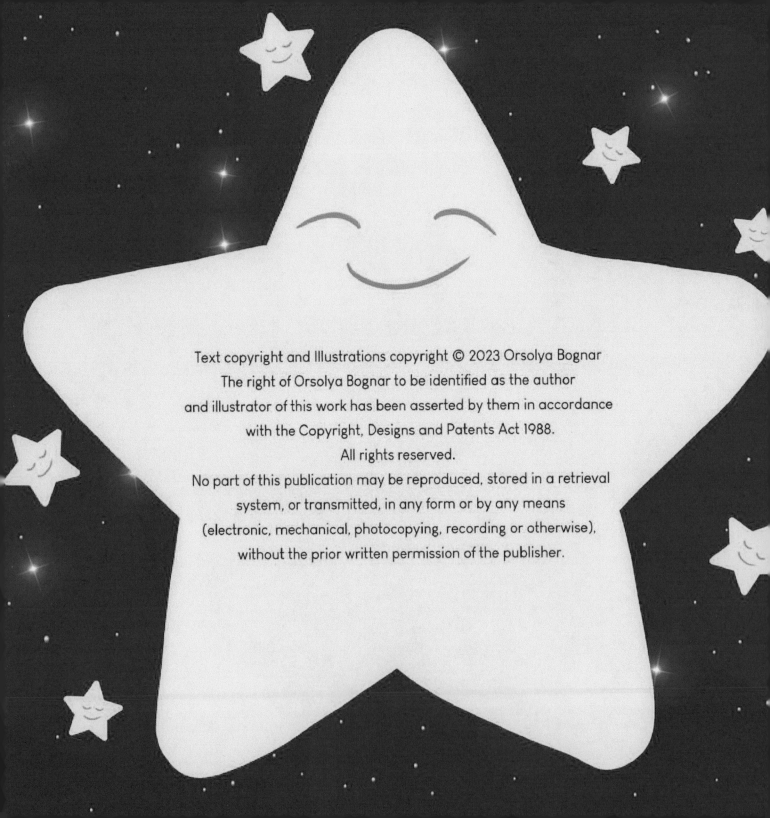

Louis the Lamb ...

Goodnight with Louis the Lamb

Orsolya Bognar

ACKNOWLEDGEMENT

I would like to express my heartfelt gratitude to all those who made
"Goodnight with Louis the Lamb" possible.
To my loving family, and to friends who inspired
the story with their unwavering support and love,
thank you for being my constant source of inspiration.
And to the young readers and their families,
thank you for embracing this story
and allowing Louis to become a part of your bedtime routines.
May his journey bring you joy, peace, and sweet dreams.

In a lush green meadow,
where the flowers grow,
Lived a little lamb named Louis,
with a coat as white as snow.

He played all day,
with a hop, a skip and a leap,
But as the sun set,
he knew it was time to sleep.

Louis made his way
to his cozy barn,
His favourite place
on the whole of the farm.

He tucked in his hay,
he felt cozy and snug,
With the quiet night
and moonlight's gentle hug.

His little eyes
began to close,
As he drifted into
a peaceful doze.

As he slept,
his little heart would swell,
With all the love he felt,
he knew everything was well.

Goodnight little Louis,
sleep so deep,
With your wool so white
and your eyes so sweet.

As he slept,
through the magical night,
The stars above twinkled
ever so bright.

We love you so much,
our little lad,
And we'll be here for you always,
your mum and dad.

As the night passed,
and the moon shone so bright,
Louis slept peacefully,
till morning's first light.

BIOGRAPHY

Orsolya BOGNAR, the talented author behind
"Goodnight with Louis the Lamb,"
has a gift for creating enchanting stories that captivate young readers.
Orsolya weaves a magical tale that celebrates the beauty of bedtime rituals
and the bond between a child and their beloved stuffed animal.
Through her vivid storytelling and tender illustrations,
Orsolya has created an adorable character in Louis the Lamb as an
ever-faithful, cuddly companion. She invites little ones to join him
on many adventures, starting with his journey to
dream-filled slumbers in the serenity of the night.

Printed in Great Britain
by Amazon